By Mary Man-Kong
Based on the original screenplay by Cliff Ruby & Elana Lesser
Illustrated by Carlotta Tormey

Special thanks to Vicki Jaeger, Monica Okazaki, Rob Hudnut, Shelley Dvi-Vardhana, Jesyca C. Durchin, Shea Wageman, Jennifer Twiner McCarron, Greg Richardson, Vera Zivny, Rene Toye, Lil Reichman, Sean Newton, Kevin Chai, Derek Toye, Pam Prostarr, Sheila Turner, and Walter P. Martishius

 A GOLDEN BOOK • NEW YORK

Published in the United States by Golden Books, an imprint of Random House Children's Books, a division of Random House, Inc., New York.
Library of Congress Control Number: 2005937747 ISBN-13: 978-0-375-83748-7 ISBN-10: 0-375-83748-5
www.goldenbooks.com www.randomhouse.com/kids
Printed in the United States of America 10 9 8 7 6 5 4 3 2 1

Once upon a time, there were a kind king and queen who had twelve beautiful daughters. The queen was a magnificent dancer, and she shared her special talent with all her children. The princesses followed in their mother's footsteps and loved to dance—especially Princess Genevieve.

When the queen passed away, the king was very sad. He raised his daughters as best he could, but he needed help.

"I love them," the king said. "But at times I don't understand them. If only their mother were here."

Knowing that the raising of his daughters called for a woman's touch, the king asked his cousin, Duchess Rowena, to come live in the castle.

"It looks as if I have my work cut out for me," observed Rowena. "What your daughters need is guidance."

The king believed that Rowena knew what was best, so he let his cousin teach his children to be proper princesses.

Rowena had always wanted to be queen, and this was her chance. The duchess planned to give her cousin tea laced with a deadly potion each day! As the king became weaker, Rowena would rule the kingdom. But first she had to pretend to help raise the princesses.

“You girls are dreadfully unprepared for royal life,” Rowena told the princesses as she fanned herself. She replaced the sisters’ beautiful gowns with drab gray dresses, took all the colorful decorations out of their bedroom, and even forbade them to dance.

“But it’s the triplets’ fifth birthday today,” Genevieve said. “We always dance on our birthdays. Mother made it a family tradition.”

“There will be no celebrating until you know how to act like royalty,” Rowena declared as she whirled out of the room.

The triplets were very upset, but their sisters had a surprise for them.

"When we turned five, Mother gave each of us a copy of her favorite story, *The Dancing Princess*," said Genevieve. "She had one made for each of us with our favorite flower on the cover."

Jocelyn, Kate, and Lacey were thrilled with their books! They listened closely as Genevieve read the story about a princess who danced on special stones, revealing a magical world filled with silver and gold trees, jeweled flowers, and beautiful music.

"Oh, I wish we could find that enchanted land," Lacey, the littlest princess, said. Just then, she stumbled, and her book slid across the floor. It landed on a stone—with the same flower painted on it!

"Girls, quick!" exclaimed Genevieve. "Get your books and see if you can match the flower on your book to a stone."

The princesses compared their books to different stones and soon found twelve perfect matches. "The stones are just like the ones in Mother's story!" Courtney exclaimed.

"And in the story, the princess danced from stone to stone to find the magical world," Genevieve added. As she gracefully leaped from one stone to another, a beautiful chime sounded.

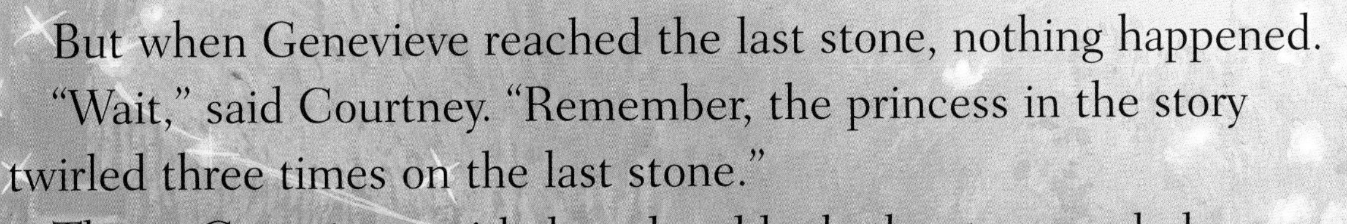

But when Genevieve reached the last stone, nothing happened.

"Wait," said Courtney. "Remember, the princess in the story twirled three times on the last stone."

Thrice Genevieve twirled, and suddenly the stone sank down, revealing a set of stairs and a doorway glowing with magical light.

Together, the sisters walked down the stairs . . .

. . . into the most beautiful world they had ever seen!

A golden boat rested on a glimmering lake. Across the water stood silver and gold trees, and beautiful jeweled flowers surrounded a golden pavilion with musical instruments.

The princesses climbed into the boat and crossed the lake. When they reached the magical pavilion, they started to dance.

"I wish we had some music," Genevieve said. No sooner had she uttered those words than a diamond flower opened and sprinkled magic dust on the instruments in the pavilion—and they began to play!

"It's amazing!" Genevieve exclaimed as she and her sisters leaped and twirled to the music.

"Ouch!" Lacey cried as she tripped and scraped her knee. "I'm always doing things like this. Why can't I be good at something?"

"You probably don't remember this," Genevieve said gently to her sister, "but Mother always told us, big or small, there's a difference only you can make." The princess dipped her handkerchief in the sparkling lake and dabbed Lacey's cut. To the girls' astonishment, the scrape disappeared before their eyes!

The princesses danced well into the night.

"It must be late," Genevieve said when she noticed that the triplets were sleeping. "And I've worn out my shoes!" Her sisters laughed as they realized that they had worn out their shoes, too.

"We'd better go home before Rowena finds out we're gone," Ashlyn said.

The princesses hated to leave, but they quickly sailed back and hurried up to their bedroom.

The next morning, all twelve princesses were so tired that they had trouble staying awake. Rowena was getting very suspicious when Derek, the royal cobbler, arrived.

Genevieve showed Derek the twelve steps she had danced the night before and twirled three times in front of him.

"It looks like someone's been having a good time," Derek said as he oiled and mended the princesses' worn shoes.

"We did," Genevieve whispered. "But I don't trust Rowena. Will you find out what she's up to?"

"I'll do my best," the cobbler promised. He secretly loved Princess Genevieve.

Meanwhile, Rowena's pet monkey, Brutus, found a pair of the princesses' worn dancing shoes and brought them to the duchess.

"They've met princes and danced the night away!" Rowena exclaimed. "If the princesses marry, my plans to be queen are ruined! We've got to stop them."

That night, Rowena ordered her henchman, Desmond, to guard the princesses' bedroom door and make sure they didn't leave. But as soon as Desmond fell asleep, Genevieve danced across the special stones.

At the golden pavilion, the sisters wished for ballet music and ballerina dresses. Magically, the flowers granted the princesses' wishes. The girls laughed and danced all night, until the soles of their shoes were worn through again.

The next morning, Desmond told Rowena that no one had gone into or come out of the princesses' bedroom. But when Rowena and Brutus entered, they found more worn dancing shoes.

"Where were you dancing last night?" Rowena snarled.

The sisters told Rowena the truth, but the duchess didn't believe them. "For lying, you shall clean the courtyard until it is spotless."

All day long, the princesses scrubbed and scrubbed. They wished their father would realize how mean Rowena was, but Rowena's poisoned tea was starting to work. The king was now very weak and asked Rowena to run the kingdom.

"Your father is sick," Rowena told the princesses. "And who can blame him for being sick? Taking care of you with your wild ways . . . Why do you think he brought me here?" The duchess then locked their bedroom door.

Heartbroken, the princesses believed that their father would get better only if they weren't around. They decided to go to the one place where they could be happy—the magical pavilion.

"I wish we could dance with handsome princes," Finna said as she danced. As soon as she uttered those words, two gold statues came to life! The girls happily danced with the handsome princes well into the morning.

Meanwhile, Derek discovered that Rowena had stolen the queen's silver goblet to buy potions. When Derek arrived to give Princess Genevieve the news, Rowena told the cobbler that the girls had run away.

Derek didn't believe Rowena. He secretly climbed up to the princesses' empty bedroom. There Derek noticed his shoe oil on certain stones in the bedroom floor. Remembering the dance steps Princess Genevieve had shown him, Derek stepped on those stones. As he reached the last stone, he turned around three times. Magically, the stone sank down, and he followed the staircase into the enchanted world.

Derek soon found Princess Genevieve. He told her about Rowena's treachery and that she was now queen.

"Rowena may not think we're proper princesses, but we *are* princesses," said Genevieve. "We can't turn our backs when things get difficult. Papa needs us." Her sisters agreed, and they hurried back to cross the glittering lake.

Back in the princesses' bedroom, Brutus had spied the cobbler descending the staircase. He shared his discovery with Rowena, and they entered the magical world.

"I wish I could see what's going on over there," Rowena said as she took out a pair of glasses. Instantly, one of the jeweled flowers sprinkled magic dust on Rowena's glasses, and they transformed into a spyglass. The duchess came up with a wicked plan. She told Brutus to pick some of the magic flowers. Then the evil duo quickly climbed back to the princesses' bedroom. Rowena commanded Desmond to smash all the magic stones!

Down in the enchanted kingdom, the magical staircase suddenly disappeared. The princesses and Derek were trapped!

Luckily, Genevieve remembered the magic flowers. "I wish to know the way out," she said. At once, the jeweled flowers sprinkled magic dust on certain stones. Genevieve danced on the stones, but nothing happened.

"Let's try together," Derek said. "May I have this dance?" As Genevieve and Derek danced across the stones together, a staircase appeared, letting them escape!

Derek and the princesses raced toward the palace. But how could they stop Rowena now that she was queen?

"We still have something Rowena doesn't," Genevieve reminded her sisters. "We have the power of twelve." While some of her sisters raced to get a doctor, Genevieve and Derek searched for the duchess.

Realizing she was cornered, Rowena pulled out one of the magic flowers. "I wish for armor to protect the queen," she said. Instantly, the flower blew magic dust on a suit of armor—and it came to life! Genevieve and Derek narrowly escaped a deadly sword before Derek smashed the armor to pieces.

"I wish you would dance your life away," Rowena shouted, using her last enchanted flower. Magic dust blew toward Genevieve and Derek, but Genevieve quickly flipped open one of Rowena's fans and waved it. The magic dust blew back toward the duchess. Suddenly, Rowena's feet started tapping, and she danced uncontrollably. "Help! Help!" Rowena cried as her dancing feet danced her far away from the castle.

Rowena was finally gone. But there was no time to waste—the king had to be saved.

"I think I can help," Lacey said. The littlest princess gave her father some water from her vial. "It's from the lake. I took some after I scraped my knee."

Slowly, the king's eyes fluttered open, and he smiled at his daughters.

"It worked!" Genevieve exclaimed.

"Where would I be without you?" the king asked his little daughter. "Your mother always told me . . ."

"Big or small, there's a difference only you can make," finished Lacey with a smile.

"And you have all made a difference," the king said as he hugged his daughters close to him.

That spring, a beautiful wedding was held at the palace. Derek married Princess Genevieve, and everyone lived—and danced—happily ever after.